FORGE NO. 11

D0801926

Emperor Mitsumune, ruler of Nayado, placed a death sentence upon the head of the monk Obo-san for his refusal to surrender the Weapon of Heaven. Obo-san and his companions Wulf and Aiko fled to the temporary safety of a northern monastery. When the army of neighboring Shinacea attacked Nayado, Obo-san used the Weapon of Heaven to destroy the invaders. Obo-san then called for his followers to return to the monastery.

Ron
MARZ
WRITER

Bart
SEARS
PENCILER

Mark
PENNINGTON
INKER

Michael
ATIYEH
COLORIST

Dave
LANPHEAR
LETTERER

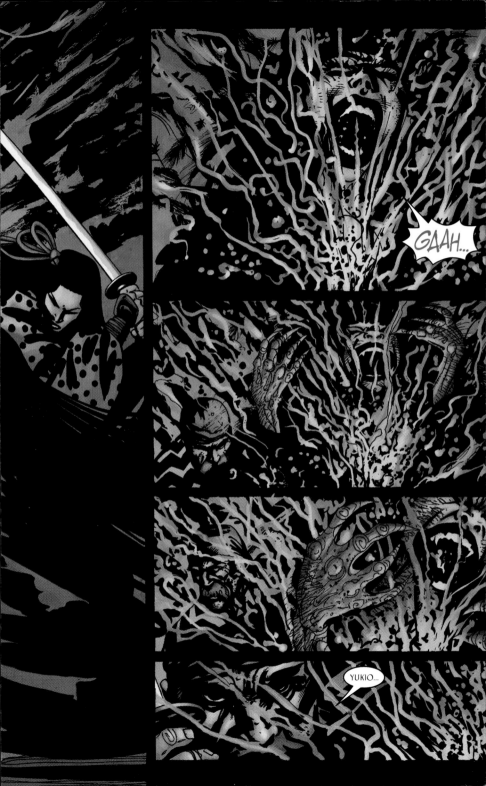

"TELL ME OF THE MONASTERY, AIKO. THEY WOULD TRULY WELCOME A *WOMAN* HERE? A WOMAN OF *MY* PAST?"

THESE ARE...CURIOUS TIMES, AYA.

TAKAIHASHI MONASTERY HAS BECOME MORE THAN A PLACE OF FAITH FOR OBO-SAN'S FELLOW MONKS. IT IS A REFUGE AGAINST MITSUMUNE'S MADNESS.

AS WULF IS WELCOMED HERE, SO TOO WILL YOU BE.

NOW THAT WE ARE TOGETHER, I WILL NOT LEAVE WULF'S SIDE.

IS THERE ANYONE FOR *YOU*, AIKO? OR DO YOU PURSUE THE WARRIOR'S WAY *ALONE?*

THERE IS...

...ONE.

BUT THERE IS SO MUCH ELSE TO CONSUME HIM...

...AND I WOULD NEVER PRESUME TO DISTRACT HIM FROM SUCH MATTERS.

IT CAN NEVER BE.

YOU *HONOR* US BY GREETING OUR RETURN, KONOSKE-SAN.

I MUST SPEAK WITH OBO-SAN. WE ENCOUNTERED THE DEMON-WITCH YUKIO AGAIN.

THEN WE ARE DOUBLY GLAD TO SEE YOU SAFELY RETURNED, WULF.

BUT I AM AFRAID OBO-SAN IS GONE.

GONE?

HE HAS DEPARTED FROM TAKAIHASHI IN ORDER TO SEEK SOLITUDE.

HE MAKES HIS WAY INTO THE MOUNTAINS...

Negation®

CHAPTER 13

KAINE

The God-Emperor CHARON conquered His chaotic universe and forged an intergalactic empire known as:

The NegaTioN

Charon now casts His baleful eye across the gulf between realities and covets the bright and thriving worlds in *our* cosmos.

On His orders, one hundred strangers were abducted from our universe and brought to His dark realm to be studied and tested on a harsh prison-world. Some captives bore a mysterious mark known as the Sigil, granting them astonishing abilities. Others were inherently powerful. Most, however, were simple, ordinary humans.

One such human named Obregon Kaine led a bloody uprising against the Negation prison warden, Komptin. The few captives who escaped along with Kaine wander the hostile stars, seeking a way home.

SAMAKAR

CHARON

KOMPTIN

Kaine and company have joined forces with a group of superhuman Australians led by a woman called Samakar. Kaine's group seeks to rescue baby Memi. Samakar's people are searching for their Atlantean ally, Gammid. Both of their lost comrades are being held captive on the Negation Throneworld by Charon and his enforcer, Lawbringer Qztr. Now the fugitives and the Australians launch a daring raid on the heart of the evil empire...

QZTR

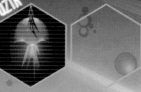

TONY BEDARD WRITER

PAUL PELLETIER PENCILER

DAVE MEIKIS INKER

JAMES ROCHELLE COLORIST

TROY PETERI LETTERER

WELL, THAT EXPLAINS HOW THEY'VE MANAGED TO HURL MURQUADE'S BROKEN FLAGSHIP AT ME, COMMANDEERING A *JUMP-GATE*, THOUGH...

...*THAT* SOUNDS LIKE THE WORK OF YOUR MOTHER'S CLEVER FRIENDS.

COO--!

EMPEROR, I HAVE A LONG-RANGE VISUAL LOCK ON KAINE'S STOLEN SHUTTLE. THEY'RE APPROACHING THE JUMP-GATE, CLOAKED IN A STEALTH-SPHERE. THEY HAVEN'T DETECTED US YET.

I KNOW YOU FORBADE ME TO KILL HIM BEFORE, BUT KAINE CAN'T POSSIBLY BE ALLOWED TO GET AWAY WITH THIS.

PERMISSION TO FIRE?

YES, KOMPTIN. FIRE AT WILL, THEN SWEEP THE WRECKAGE ONCE YOU'VE DESTROYED THE SHIP.

PICK UP THIS CHILD'S MOTHER-- PRISONER *ZAIDA*. IF SHE'S ANYTHING LIKE HER OFFSPRING, SHE'LL HAVE *SURVIVED* WHATEVER YOU THROW AT HER.

FATHER, I CAN FEEL THE AUSTRALIANS UP THERE, HIDDEN WITHIN THE COMMAND SHIP.

PLEASE LET *ME* KILL THEM FOR YOU.

PATIENCE, QZTR. OUR DEFENSES HERE HAVE NEVER BEEN CHALLENGED.

THIS SHOULD PROVE... *ENLIGHTENING.*

BUT, *FATHER--!* THROWING OUR OWN FLAGSHIP AT THE *THRONEWORLD!* THE...THE *INSULT* IS *UNENDURABLE!*

TRY TO REMEMBER TO WHOM YOU SPEAK. I AM *BEYOND* INSULT.

WHAT DO I CARE WHAT MY SUBJECTS THINK OF ME? IF I DESIRED IT, COULD I NOT *SNUFF OUT* EVERY LIFE IN THE REALM?

...

QZTR...?

...YES, FATHER. FORGIVE ME. THE THOUGHT OF ACTUALLY *DOING* SUCH A THING... IT'S...

...IT'S *INTOXICATING.*

OH, QZTR. WHATEVER WILL I DO WITH YOU...?

COME, MY SOLDIERS ARE TEACHING THESE INVADERS WHAT IT MEANS TO DEFY THE NEGATION. LET'S ENJOY THE SHOW...

RIGHT NOW, A LOT OF YOU ARE WONDERING IF WE'RE *CURSED*. YOU'RE THINKING, "WHY *ME?* WHY *US?*"
WHY WERE WE LEFT BEHIND BACK ON EARTH, WHEN THE REST OF HUMANITY DEPARTED FOR *GODHOOD?*
WHY, WHEN IT SEEMED WE COULD FOLLOW IN THEIR FOOTSTEPS, DID WE END UP IN *THIS* HELLISH PLACE?
WHY WERE WE GIVEN SUCH *POWER,* ONLY TO BE NEARLY DRIVEN *MAD* BY IT?
AND *WHY* DOES IT FALL TO US NOW TO *SACRIFICE* OURSELVES AGAINST THE MOST POWERFUL FOE IMAGINABLE?
THIS MOMENT IS WHY! ALL OUR PAST SUFFERING *STRENGTHENED* US FOR THIS! THE FATE OF TWO UNIVERSES IS *OURS* TO DECIDE!

SO LET'S *STRIKE* WITHOUT *FEAR!* LET'S *HURT* THEM SO BAD THEY'LL NEVER SEE KAINE'S SHIP SLIPPING PAST THEIR DEFENSES!

LET'S MAKE CERTAIN THEY DON'T NOTICE GAMMID'S RESCUE UNTIL IT'S TOO LATE...

"...BECAUSE ONCE THE *ATLANTEAN* IS FREE, *NOTHING* CAN STOP US!"

HOW DID YOU *KNOW*...?

I'LL EXPLAIN LATER. WE'LL *ALL* HAVE SOME EXPLAINING TO DO LATER.

RIGHT NOW WE'VE GOT TO HIT KOMPTIN *HARD* BEFORE HE KNOWS--

--WHAT'S *HAPPENING*?! THEY WERE RIGHT *IN FRONT* OF US!

I DON'T KNOW, SIR!

OF COURSE, YOU DON'T! AS LONG AS THEIR STEALTH-SPHERE'S ENGAGED, OUR ONLY CHANCE IS A *VISUAL*--

KANGG

WHAT IN THE--?

SIR! THEY'VE LOCKED ON A DOCKING TUBE!

I HAVE *EARS*, SOLDIER! *SEAL* THE CABIN AND STAND BY TO *REPEL BOARDERS!*

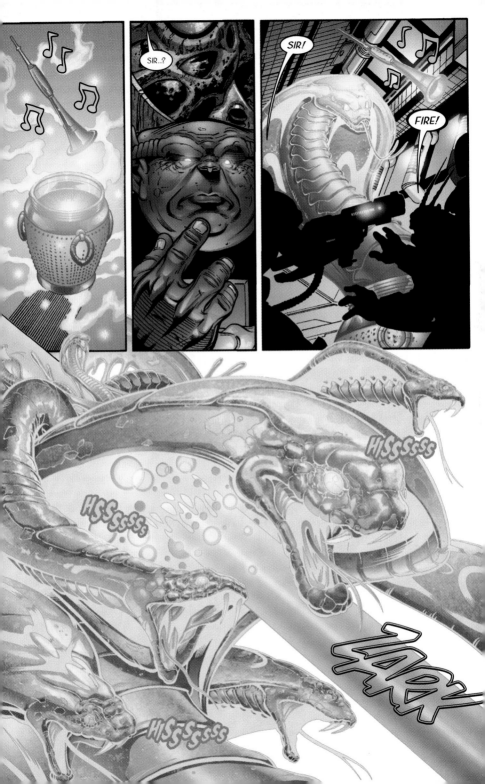

IT'S GOTTEN PRETTY *QUIET* IN THERE.

I THINK IT'S PROBABLY *SAFE* TO GO IN.

CAN YOU CRACK THE COMBINATION?

I'VE YET TO MEET THE LOCK I CAN'T *PICK*...

BEEP BEE DOOP

MATUA, YOU *DIDN'T*--!

THEY'RE JUST *SLEEPING.*

NEGATION SPACE IS STILL KEEPING ALL MY *ATTACK SPELLS* SCRAMBLED UP, BUT I'VE MANAGED TO GET A FEW *DEFENSIVE* ONES WORKING RIGHT.

YOU'RE GONNA BE SOME *BIG GUN* ONCE YOU SOLVE THAT LITTLE PROBLEM.

LOCK THESE GUYS UP IN THE CARGO HOLD. SAMAKAR'S PEOPLE WON'T LAST LONG IF WE DON'T DO *OUR* PART ASAP.

WE'RE NOT GONNA FINISH THEM OFF? YOU MUST BE *JOKING!*

DO YOU THINK FOR A MINUTE ONCE KOMPTIN RECOVERS THAT *HE'LL* EVER STOP HUNTING *US?*

COME ON, KAINE! YOU'VE ALWAYS DONE THE SMART THING UP UNTIL *NOW...!*

SOMETIMES THE *SMART* MOVE IS THE VERY *WORST* MOVE YOU CAN MAKE.

I HAD MY *FILL* OF COLD-BLOODED MURDER BACK IN THE ARMY. *NEVER AGAIN.*

FORGET YOU. I'M PUTTING THIS MANIAC OUT OF OUR MISERY.

YOU DO THAT, DRAKE, AND YOU MAKE AN *ENEMY* OUT OF *ME.*

IS THAT *REALLY* WHAT YOU WANT?

WHEN THE TIME COMES, I WON'T SAY *"I TOLD YOU SO."* I'LL JUST BREAK YOUR JAW...

IF THIS CARGO HOLD'S *FULL*, WE TOSS THEM OUT THE AIRLOCK.

NOW, NOW...

WHAT IN THE WORLDS...?

O-KAY...

NO REACTION AT ALL. MAYBE IT'S *SLEEPING*.

MAYBE WE'LL GET LUCKY AND IT'LL *EAT* THESE GUYS.

AND BITE THE HAND THAT FEEDS IT...?

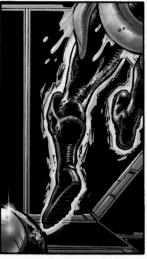

A HIGH CASTELLAN NAMED KOMPTIN REQUESTS PERMISSION TO *LAND.* HE SAYS HE'S BRINGING PRISONERS FOR THE EMPEROR.

NO VISUAL CONFIRMATION, BUT HIS SECURITY CODES CHECK OUT.

SIR, THE *CLARION* IS NO LONGER A COLLISION THREAT, BUT THE *ATTACKERS* AREN'T GOING DOWN EASY!

MOBILIZE GROUND TROOPS-- SECURE THE IMPERIAL PALACE!

YEAH, YEAH. CLEAR HIM AND GET BACK TO TELEMETRY!

AT LEAST *SOMEONE'S* BRINGING GOOD NEWS...!

THEY FELL FOR IT.

GOOD WORK. NOW, ONE LAST THING...

...SHOW ME HOW TO *FLY* THIS THING--JUST THE *BASICS.* WEAPONS CONTROL, TOO. THEN YOU GET BACK TO THE SHUTTLE WITH THE *OTHERS.*

IN FIVE MINUTES? *IMPOSSIBLE.* BEST I CAN DO IS AUTOMATE A LANDING SEQUENCE AND PUT THE GUNS ON MANUAL. WHAT'VE YOU GOT IN MIND?

I WANNA GIVE YOU A REALISTIC SHOT AT RESCUING THE *BABY...*

CHAPTER 21

THEY WERE THE ATLANTEANS,

a peaceful civilization of artists and philosophers who used their
phenomenal mental and physical skills to build an island utopia. They had but one responsibility:
to guide and shepherd Earth's newborn race of *homo sapiens* towards a grand and glorious destiny.
But when a mysterious cataclysm plunged Atlantis and its people beneath the waves, six – and only
six – were awakened by a nameless stranger one thousand centuries later to find their utopia forgotten
and in ruins, their brothers and sisters caught in an unshakeable slumber...and the human race gone,
having vanished centuries ago in the Transition, a passage to a higher plane of existence.

Having concluded their adventure with Gannish and Yala, the Atlanteans make their way home. But,
unbeknownst to them, Aristophanes plans to change the destiny of the sleeping Atlanteans and the world
they live in. Only the bestial Thraxis suspects the truth...

The mental and physical abilities of the Atlanteans are identical in nature but not in application.
Capricia and her teammates have each channeled their abilities into different skills:

CAPRICIA	DANIK	TUG	ZEPHYRE	GALVAN	VERITYN
Shapeshifter and empath	Keeper of the secrets	Telekinetic strongman	Hypermetabolic intellectual	Manipulator of the electromagnetic spectrum	Seer of all truths

Chuck
DIXON
WRITER

Ivan
REIS
Guest PENCILER

Rick
MAGYAR
INKER

Roland
PARIS
INKER

Andrew
CROSSLEY
Guest COLORIST

Dave
LANPHEAR
LETTERER

I WILL **NOT** HAVE MY WILL THWARTED!

NOT BY **YOU,** CREATURE!

MY BLADE--

FORGED IN THE FIRES OF THEBREBUS.

HAMMERED FROM RAW STEEL--

--IN A CEREMONY OLDER THAN THIS CITY.

I THOUGHT ONCE I GOT *WITH* YOU GUYS ALL MY QUESTIONS WOULD BE ANSWERED.

BUT I'M *STILL* AS CLUELESS AS I WAS WHEN TERRA COGNITO ABANDONED ME HERE.

YOU *REALLY* WANT TO KNOW!

SURE?

WELL, *YEAH.*

SURE.

THRAXIS IS AN *ALIEN* FROM A RACE OF CREATURES WHO WERE ARTIFICIALLY EVOLVED TO SERVE *ANOTHER* RACE OF ALIENS CALLED "THE MASTERS." *THEY* CAME HERE A LONG TIME AGO AND FOUGHT OUR ANCIENT ATLANTEAN ANCESTORS WHO WERE LED BY A GUY NAMED ARISTOPHANES. THRAXIS AND ARISTOPHANES WERE PUT IN STASIS LIKE A HUNDRED THOUSAND YEARS AGO, BUT THEY'RE *AWAKE* NOW. OKAY!

SORRY I *ASKED.*

IT'S A LOT TO TAKE IN ALL AT ONCE.

YOU'LL *UNDERSTAND* THE STORY BETTER--

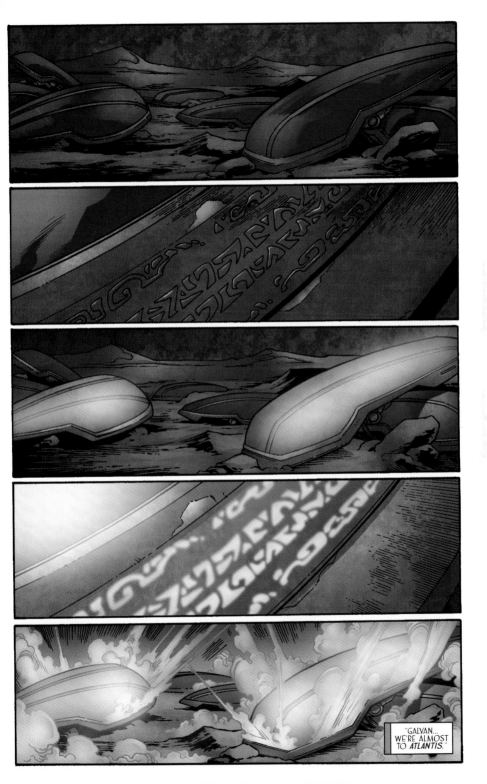

"GALVAN...
WE'RE ALMOST
TO *ATLANTIS.*"

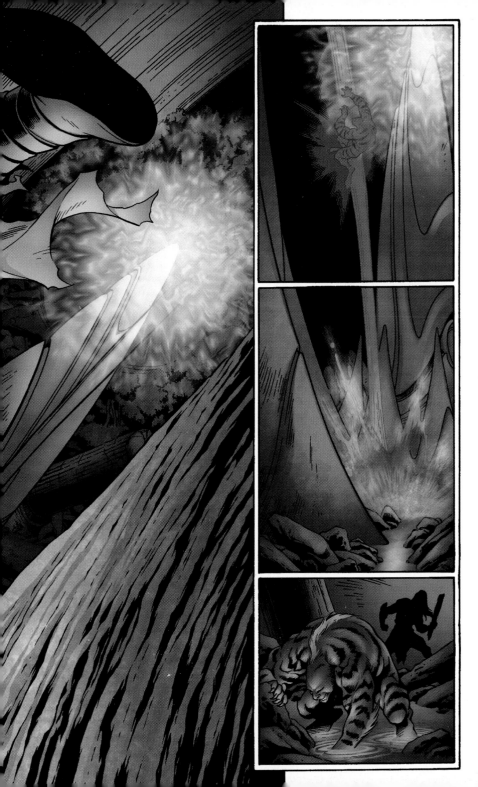

DIE!

DIE THE DEATH SO *LONG* OVERDUE!

THE *LAST* OF YOUR KIND!

ONCE I HAVE *DESTROYED* YOU--

≈ARNH!≈

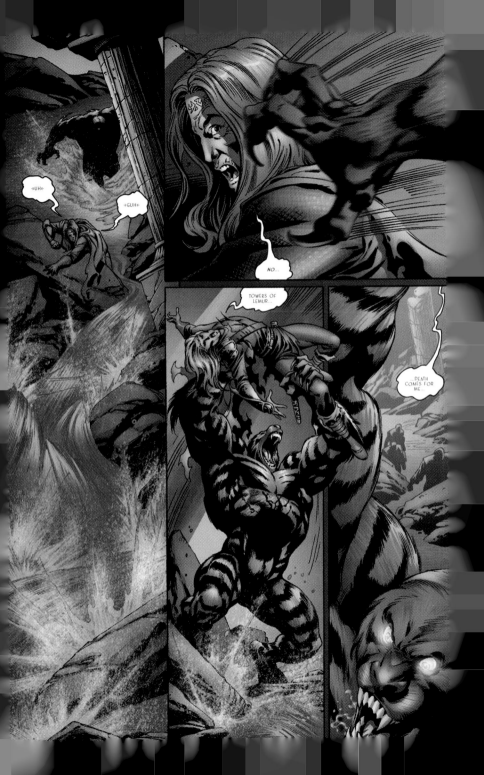

MERIDIAN

®

CHAPTER 31

Far away on the world of Demetria,

explosions rocked the surface and gigantic rocks shot into the sky and stayed there. Settlers established great city-states on these ore-buoyant islands, using floating ships to move between them.

One of these islands is Meridian, home of shipbuilders and Sephie. Sephie has become the Minister of Meridian after her father Turos' death. Her uncle Ilahn is the Minister of the rich city-state of Cadador, which controls most of the shipping and trade on Demetria.

A mysterious force has endowed both Sephie and Ilahn with power – opposing forces – Ilahn's destruction versus Sephie's renewal.

Ilahn wants to control Sephie – and Meridian – but Sephie has been fighting to resist Ilahn's control of herself and Demetria's commerce. The conflict between them erupts into a battle, during which Ilahn disappears... apparently dead at Sephie's hands.

Sephie departs for Cadador to establish her rule in Ilahn's absence. She is not greeted with open arms, but after a show of power, is granted a grudging respect. Political wheels turn, however, and Cadador's councilors force Sephie to acknowledge that she, an unmarried orphan, must now concentrate on providing an heir for both Cadador and Meridian. Since Sephie believes her childhood love Jad is dead, she resigns herself to a loveless marriage.

Refugees from the island of Torbel, destroyed by Ilahn's callous decision, tried to claim Cadador in repayment. Sephie negotiated a settlement: the Torbellians were to be given a new island and promises of work. Sephie is left believing that she can now get on with the business of governing Cadador, but her method of negotiation has angered the Cadadorian council. They will do anything to get rid of their new Minister.

Barbara **KESEL**
WRITER

June **BRIGMAN**
Guest PENCILER

Drew **GERACI**
Guest INKER

Richard & Tanya **HORIE**
Guest COLORISTS

Troy **PETERI**
LETTERER

I had become the Minister of Cadador through fraud, claiming to have killed a man I know to be alive.

My uncle, Ilahn.

My lie a heavy weight, the ship of my spirit might have sunk if not buoyed by the certainty that the two islands I governed and the world I had vowed to protect were best served by my deceit.

I was becoming adept at the business of telling untruths.

Navigating a course of lies makes for an uncomfortable journey.

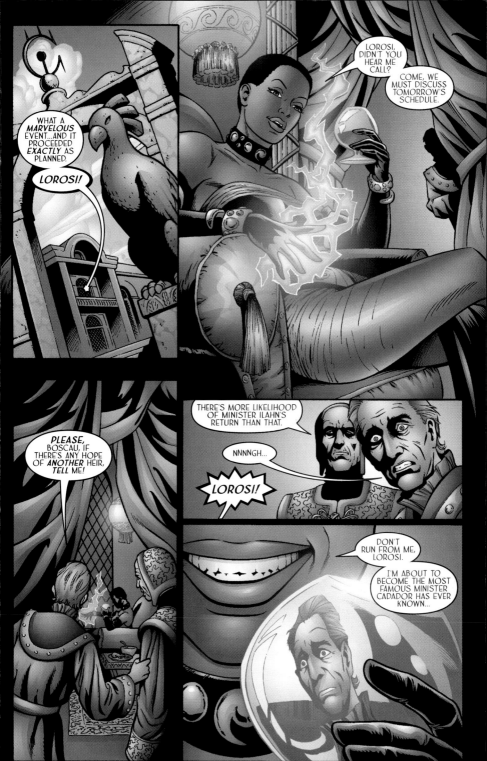

SO WHERE ARE WE HEADED, SEPHIE?

MERIDIAN?

YES, BUT WITH TWO STOPS BEFORE.

I WAS THINKING ABOUT THE TORBELLIANS AND THE CHALLENGES FACING THEM ON THEIR NEW ISLAND.

THERE'S GOT TO BE A WAY TO HELP THEM PROSPER.

THEN THERE'S A PROMISE I MADE AND INTEND TO KEEP...

...AND THERE MAY BE A WAY TO INTERTWINE THE TWO.

THAT'S THE ALBUM OF YOUR MOTHER'S PAINTINGS?

WILL YOU BE SHARING HER ART WITH THE REST OF US?

AAAAH... CRENNER, I...

IT'S KIND OF... PRIVATE.

OH, A LIKE A DIARY.

THAT'S FINE.

THANK YOU FOR BEING SO... UNDERSTANDING, CRENNER.

SEPHIE, YOU NEVER KNEW YOUR MOTHER.

YOU'RE ENTITLED TO KEEP PART OF HER TO YOURSELF.

JUST DON'T KEEP *EVERYTHING* INSIDE...

Our Story So Far...

Arwyn

he dread warlord Mordath was slain more than three centuries ago, pierced by an arrow shot from the bow of the legendary warrior Ayden. Ayden retreated to the solitude from which he'd come, but broke the fatal arrow into Five Fragments and scattered them to Quin's Five Lands, promising to return should the pieces ever be reunited.

Gareth

Now Mordath has risen from his tomb. Aided by a sigil that allows him to create and command fire, Mordath has again conquered the Five Lands. One woman, the archer Arwyn, survived her city's destruction at the hands of Mordath's troll armies. Her husband and daughter did not.

Bohr

Swearing vengeance, Arwyn has taken up the quest to reunite the Five Fragments at the behest of a mysterious and apparently magical woman calling herself Neven. Armed with Ayden's bow and accompanied by the adventurer Gareth and her dog Kreeg, Arwyn has dedicated herself to bringing about Mordath's destruction.

Koht

After obtaining the First Fragment in Middelyn, Arwyn and Gareth journeyed to Ankhara, home to a race of winged warriors, where they joined the rebellion against Mordath's occupying trolls. Arwyn and Gareth allowed themselves to be captured in order to lure the trolls into a trap. However, as the trap was sprung and the battle for the city began, Gareth was hurled from the cliffs and Arwyn was given over to her troll pursuer, Bohr.

 Ron **MARZ** WRITER

 Greg **LAND** PENCILER

 Jay **LEISTEN** INKER

 Justin **PONSOR** COLORIST

 Troy **PETERI** LETTERER

LET GO OF ME!

GARETH!

GARETH?

PULL HER BACK FROM THE EDGE.

I DON'T WANT HER *PITCHING HERSELF OFF* AFTER HER BOYFRIEND...

...SHE'S TOO VALUABLE *ALIVE.*

GET HER READY. WE'RE LEAVING.

YOU *FILTH!* IT WASN'T SUPPOSED TO *BE* LIKE THIS!

HE *TOLD* YOU WHAT YOU WANTED TO KNOW AND YOU KILLED HIM ANYWAY!

UNTRUE. CAPTAIN BOHR HAD NOTHING TO DO WITH YOUR COMPANION'S DEATH.

I ORDERED HIM KILLED AFTER HE REVEALED THE WHEREABOUTS OF THE REBELS. HE WAS NO LONGER OF *USE* TO ME.

I'LL SEE YOU *DEAD,* KOHT. I SWEAR TO YOU I WILL.

I FIND THAT *UNLIKELY.*

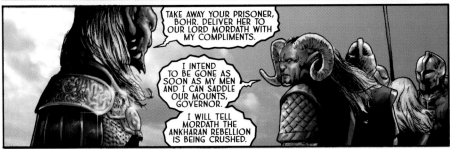

TAKE AWAY YOUR PRISONER, BOHR. DELIVER HER TO OUR LORD MORDATH WITH MY COMPLIMENTS.

I INTEND TO BE GONE AS SOON AS MY MEN AND I CAN SADDLE OUR MOUNTS, GOVERNOR.

I WILL TELL MORDATH THE ANKHARAN REBELLION IS BEING CRUSHED.

IT WILL *BE* CRUSHED LONG BEFORE YOU REACH MIDDELYN.

NOW THAT WE KNOW WHERE THE REBELS HAVE BEEN HIDING...

"...MY TROOPS WILL *SLAUGHTER* EVERY LAST ONE OF THEM."

AAGH!

HUNT THEM DOWN!

HUNT DOWN OUR OPPRESSORS AND *SLAY* THEM!

GHRG!

WE ARE LURED INTO A *TRAP!*

RETREAT!

RETR—

EVERY LAST ONE OF THEM.

THE TROLLS FLEE BACK TO THE STREETS IN *TERROR,* DAWN WARRIOR.

AS WE KNEW THEY WOULD.

THE PLAN SUCCEEDS.

OUR ALLIES WERE ABLE TO LEAD THE TROLLS TO US...

"...NOW WE MUST FREE *THEM* FROM THE CLUTCHES OF OUR ENEMIES."

MIND YOUR *CHARGE,* KNECHT.

SHE'D SOONER SLIT YOUR THROAT THAN LOOK AT YOU, AND SHE'S WELL ABLE TO *DO* IT GIVEN HALF A CHANCE.

NOW THAT WE FINALLY *HAVE* HER, WE CAN ILL AFFORD TO LOSE HER.

IF WE RIDE *HARD* WE CAN BE BACK AT MORDATH'S FORTRESS WITHIN A WEEK. AND WE DELIVER NOT ONLY THE *WOMAN* TO OUR MASTER...

...BUT *AYDEN'S BOW* AS WELL.

CAPTAIN, IS THIS TRULY THE—

HLLK!

THUK

ARWYN!

TIYE...

WE'RE NOT LEAVING YOU TO THEIR MERCIES.

MY *BOW!*

MAKE SURE MY *BOW* ISN'T LEFT BEHIND!

WE *NEED* YOU...

...AND YOUR WEAPON.

STOP THEM!

STOP THEM BEFORE THEY...

WHERE IS THE OTHER?

GARETH.

WHERE HAVE YOU *BEEN?!* YOU WERE SUPPOSED TO *RESCUE* US!

KOHT THREW GARETH FROM THE CLIFFS. WE HAVE TO GO *BACK* FOR HIM!

WE HAVE TO GO BACK!

...GET AWAY.

WE'RE LUCKY TO HAVE FOUND YOU AT ALL. WE MEANT TO REACH YOU SOONER, BUT WE NEVER SUSPECTED KOHT WOULD TAKE YOU TO THE CLIFFS.

NO ONE SURVIVES THAT FALL.

GARETH, MORE THAN ANYONE, KNEW THE RISKS OF PERPETRATING THIS RUSE.

NO, THERE HAS TO BE A *CHANCE*. HE COULD HAVE—

IF YOUR FRIEND WAS HURLED FROM THE CLIFFS, HE IS *DEAD*.

GOING BACK TO FIND HIS CORPSE WILL SERVE NO PURPOSE.

I'M SORRY, ARWYN.

WE HAVE TO RETURN TO THE CITY...

RAHM!

ARWYN?

WHERE IS GARETH?

DEAD.

YOU DIDN'T REACH US IN TIME.

I AM SORRY. WE DID TRY.

HRUFF

KREEG...

...I'M HAPPY TO SEE YOU TOO, BOY.

I REGRET YOUR FRIEND'S DEATH, ARWYN.

IT WAS HIS PLAN THAT ALLOWED US THIS OPPORTUNITY...

...BUT YOU'LL AT LEAST HAVE YOUR CHANCE AT REVENGE.

YES...

"THE STREETS RUN *RED* WITH YOUR BLOOD. YOUR *DEAD* LITTER THE GROUND..."

"...WHILE *MY PEOPLE* FLY FREE. THE BATTLE IS *ENDED*..."

...AND OUR CITY AGAIN *BELONGS* TO US.

YOU ARE THE *ONE?*

YOU ARE THIS *DAWN WARRIOR* WHO LEADS THEM?

I AM. I AM THE *PROTECTOR* OF MY PEOPLE. I AM THE *BANE* OF OUR ENEMIES.

MY MEN *ARE* DEAD. BUT THIS IS NOT YET *OVER*...

...NOT WHILE *I* STILL DRAW BREATH.

I WON'T BEG FOR YOUR *MERCY*.

I WASN'T *OFFERING* IT.

THE FRAGMENT.

HIDDEN WITHIN THE DAWN SWORD'S *HILT* ALL THIS TIME.

THIS *IS* WHAT YOU WERE SEEKING.

YES.

YOU AIDED US WHEN IT WOULD HAVE BEEN FAR EASIER FOR YOU TO MOVE ON.

IN *SETTING ASIDE* YOUR QUEST, YOU GAINED THE *OBJECT* OF YOUR QUEST.

INDEED, YOU ARE THE *FAVORED* OF THE GODS.

THIS IS *YOURS*.

BUT...

...IF AYDEN'S FRAGMENT GAVE THE DAWN SWORD ITS *POWER*...

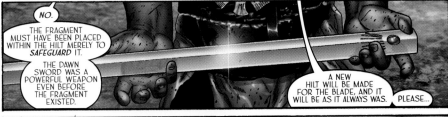

NO.

THE FRAGMENT MUST HAVE BEEN PLACED WITHIN THE HILT MERELY TO *SAFEGUARD* IT.

THE DAWN SWORD WAS A POWERFUL WEAPON EVEN BEFORE THE FRAGMENT EXISTED.

A NEW HILT WILL BE MADE FOR THE BLADE, AND IT WILL BE AS IT ALWAYS WAS.

PLEASE...

...*TAKE* THE FRAGMENT.

THANK YOU.

ALL IT COST WAS GARETH'S LIFE.

I GRIEVE THAT YOUR FRIEND WAS LOST. HE HAS BEEN *AVENGED*...

...BUT I KNOW THAT DOES NOT LESSEN YOUR PAIN.

YOU *CAN* STAY WITH US, ARWYN. WE DO NOT ACCEPT OUTSIDERS EASILY, BUT YOU HAVE *EARNED* A PLACE HERE.

NOW THAT WE HAVE TAKEN OUR LAND'S CAPITAL, THE REBELLION CAN SPREAD TO OTHER CITIES IN ANKHARA. YOU WOULD BE A *BOON* TO OUR CAUSE.

I'M FLATTERED THAT YOUR PEOPLE WOULD ACCEPT ME, RAHM. BUT I *SWORE* I WOULD SEE MORDATH DESTROYED...

...AND I DO NOT BELIEVE THAT WILL HAPPEN BY SIMPLE INSURRECTION.

I MUST CONTINUE MY QUEST, NOW MORE THAN EVER. I HAVE *TWO* OF THE FIVE FRAGMENTS...

...BUT *EACH* WAS BOUGHT WITH A LIFE.

THEN CAN ONE OF MY WARRIORS *ACCOMPANY* YOU?

IT'S THE *LEAST* WE OWE YOU.

I APPRECIATE YOUR KINDNESS, RAHM...

...BUT THUS FAR THOSE WHO HAVE *HELPED* ME HAVE COME TO DIRE ENDS. I WON'T DOOM ANY *OTHERS* TO THAT FATE.

I'LL STAY IN ANKHARA ONLY LONG ENOUGH TO GATHER SUPPLIES AND FIND A MOUNT. THEN I CONTINUE SOUTH TOWARD OUDUBAI.

THIS QUEST MUST BE MINE...

REPORT.

THE CITY IS *LOST*, MY CAPTAIN.

THE REBELS HAVE SLAIN NEARLY *ALL* OF THE OCCUPIERS, INCLUDING GOVERNOR KOHT.

I BARELY MANAGED TO ESCAPE WITH MY LIFE.

IT WAS WISE OF YOU TO KEEP OUR FORCE OUTSIDE THE WALLS. *WE* SURELY WOULD HAVE BEEN SLAUGHTERED AS WELL.

WHAT NOW? WHAT OF OUR *QUARRY?*

BOUND FOR OUDUBAI, I'M CERTAIN.

SHE'LL DEPART VIA THE CITY'S SOUTH GATE. SHE LIKELY ALREADY *HAS.*

WE'LL HAVE TO FIND A WAY AROUND. THE WOMAN WILL GAIN *DAYS* ON US...

...BUT THE *CHASE* IS FAR FROM OVER.

CHAPTER 6

Greetings From... STONE RIVER

Touring Stone River with Boxcar Berkely.

Community Service at MealsMobile.

Local Artist Signs His Work.

NATIONAL BUREAU of INVESTIGATION
*****URGENT BULLETIN*****

Attention all Field Agents in the states of Gossmer, Millston, Arroba, and Welkin:

Reports from Stone River, Gossmer, indicate that Most Wanted Fugitive Cassandra Starkweather has struck again. Three employees of Stone River Hospital were killed last night in the hospital's "MealsMobile" office. Subject Starkweather was witnessed departing the scene.

Starkweather's total known body count now stands at nine. Her murder spree began at a sanitarium in Welkin, where she killed three staffers before escaping. She is also believed responsible for the deaths of two ambulance drivers and the son of the sheriff in Tucker, Gossmer.

Starkweather is believed to have fled Tucker by rail. Agents working the "Railsplitter" slayings are advised to search train routes passing near Stone River.

All agents are reminded that Starkweather is mentally unstable. She claims her victims are supernatural monsters disguised as humans. She also appears to target healthcare workers. She is presumed armed and dangerous.

Special Agent Gunnar Melchior, in charge of the Starkweather case, is en route to Stone River. Please forward all information related to this investigation to him.

****

N.B.I. Central Dispatch

Terry BEDARD *Writer*

Karl MOLINE *Penciler*

John DELL *Inker*

Nick BELL *Colorist*

Troy PETERI *Letterer*

"*J. ELGAR PURVIS* PUT ME IN CHARGE OF THIS CASE."

"IN *THIS* BUSINESS, THAT'S AS GOOD AS *GOD HIMSELF* HANDING YOU THE FLAMING SWORD AND SENDING YOU OUT TO SMITE THE WICKED."

"SOME PEOPLE AT HEADQUARTERS *QUESTION* THAT DECISION. THEY THINK I'M *TOO CLOSE* TO THESE CRIMES TO VIEW THEM OBJECTIVELY."

"I SUPPOSE THEY HAVE A *POINT*..."

"...AFTER ALL, MY OWN *FATHER* WAS ONE OF HER FIRST VICTIMS."

"BUT THERE'S A *REASON* J. ELGAR'S BEEN RUNNING THE N.B.I. EVER SINCE THE GREAT WAR. THE OLD MAN'S *NO FOOL*...

"...HE *KNOWS* THAT IF THIS GIRL'S KILLING SPREE ISN'T ENDED SOON, IT COULD SPARK A NATIONAL *PANIC*.

"SO HE PICKED *ME*, BECAUSE I'LL CHASE EVERY *LEAD*, CALL IN EVERY *FAVOR*, AND DESTROY *ANYONE* WHO KEEPS ME FROM *SNARING* THAT LITTLE *LUNATIC*.

GUNNAR MELCHIOR, MD, PhD
Special Agent-Profiler
Provisional Director
Criminal Psychology Unit
NATIONAL BUREAU of INVESTIGATION

N.B.I.

"I'VE FOLLOWED HER TRAIL THROUGH FOUR STATES, AND INTERVIEWED EVERYONE WHO'S CROSSED HER PATH. EVERYONE STILL *ALIVE*, THAT IS..."

OFFICER, YOU ARE TALKING ABOUT A *MENTAL PATIENT* WITH LESS REGARD FOR TAKING A HUMAN LIFE THAN YOU AND I WOULD HAVE FOR SWATTING A *FLY*.

I CAN ASSURE YOU THERE IS *NOTHING* GLAMOROUS ABOUT HER.

NOW, MAKE YOURSELF *USEFUL* AND HELP FIND THE MURDER WEAPON. IT SHOULD BE SIX TO EIGHT INCHES LONG, EXTREMELY *SHARP* AND *POINTY*.

TRY NOT TO GET YOUR OWN FINGERPRINTS ON ANYTHING WHILE YOU'RE AT IT.

AGENT MELCHIOR! A TIP JUST CAME IN--SOMEONE SPOTTED THE *VAN* PARKED UNDER A BRIDGE TWENTY MILES OUTSIDE OF TOWN!

OFFICER, STAY HERE AND PRESERVE THE CRIME SCENE!

LET'S GO, *FINNEY!* WE FIND THE *TRUCK,* WE FIND THE *GIRL!*

EVEN IF I WERE *ALLOWED* TO FIGHT YOUR BATTLES, I WOULDN'T *CHOOSE* TO.

THE POWER IS ALREADY *WITHIN* YOU TO DESTROY YOUR ENEMIES, CASSANDRA. I WOULDN'T KEEP YOU FROM REALIZING THIS FOR YOURSELF.

THOUGH I *WOULD* QUESTION YOUR CHOICE OF *COMPANIONS*...

HE'S GOT ME *FIGHTING BACK*, AND...AND HE CAN *SEE* THROUGH THEIR DISGUISES, JUST LIKE *ME!*

WHO... *BERKELY?* TOO-TOO, HE'S A GODSEND!

IS THAT *SO?*

YES! HE KNEW THE *DELIVERY GUY* AT THAT OLD LADY'S HOUSE WAS REALLY ONE OF THEM.

ARE YOU *SURE* HE WASN'T JUST TELLING YOU WHAT YOU WANTED TO HEAR?

...HE *KNOWS* WHEN THEY'RE BAD INSIDE. HE KNOWS THE *ENEMY.*

JUST LIKE ME.

IF YOU KNOW SOMETHING ABOUT HIM, THEN *SAY SO!* JUST DON'T MAKE ME *DOUBT* EVERY- THING! IT'S TOUGH *ENOUGH* WONDERING IF I'M *CRAZY* HALF THE TIME!

HE'S...LIKE ME. HE'S GOT THE *GIFT.* MAYBE HE DIDN'T HAVE YOU TO *JUMP-START* IT, BUT HE CAN SEE PAST THE *SURFACE* OF A PERSON...

CHECK THE VAN, FINNEY.

YES, SIR.

WELL, THIS IS ALMOST ANTI-CLIMACTIC.

YOU PEOPLE COPS? OR ARE YOU WITH... *THEM?*

AGENT MELCHIOR! THERE APPEARS TO BE ANOTHER *BODY* IN THE VAN!

LOOK FOR *IDENTIFICATION!*

AGENT... MELCHIOR...?

GUNNAR MELCHIOR, N.B.I.

SHOCKING, ISN'T IT? THAT THE MAN YOU KILLED BACK AT THE SANITARIUM MIGHT ACTUALLY HAVE A *SON.*

BUT THEN, SOCIOPATHS LIKE YOU NEVER CONSIDER YOUR VICTIMS *PEOPLE...* WITH *LIVES...* AND *FAMILIES...*

Uh, AGENT MELCHIOR? WE HAVE A *PROBLEM*...

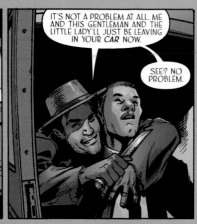

IT'S NOT A PROBLEM AT ALL. ME AND THIS GENTLEMAN AND THE LITTLE LADY'LL JUST BE LEAVING IN YOUR *CAR* NOW.

SEE? NO PROBLEM.

I'M AFRAID I CAN'T LET THAT HAPPEN.

SHOOT, MELCHIOR. FORGET ABOUT ME--JUST *SHOOT* HIM!

THAT'S ABOUT *ENOUGH* OUT OF YOU...

ah--!

OKAY! EASE UP WITH THAT *BLADE!* I'LL...

I'LL PLAY IT *YOUR* WAY, MISTER... BUT *ONLY* IF YOU AGREE TO ONE SMALL *SUBSTITUTION*...

IT'S A TERM BEHAVIORAL EXPERTS PREFER TO THE MORE COMMONLY USED *"PSYCHOPATH."*

IN SHORT, IT MEANS YOUR COMPANION IS PRONE TO *ANTISOCIAL BEHAVIOR* AND PUTS NO VALUE IN THE LIVES OF *OTHERS.*

S'FUNNY. I'VE FOUND HER TO BE RATHER *DELIGHTFUL* COMPANY.

I'M NOT SURE IF THAT SAYS MORE ABOUT *HER...* OR *YOU.*

HOLD ON, MISTER HEAD-SHRINKER. BEFORE YOU PUT OL' BERKELY UNDER THE MICROSCOPE, FINISH UP YOUR DIAGNOSIS OF MISS CASSIE.

TO BE HONEST, I DON'T KNOW YET. IS SHE A TRUE *SERIAL MURDERER,* OR JUST A *SPREE KILLER?*

THE *DIFFERENCE* BEING...?

THE SPREE KILLER EMBARKS ON ONE CONTINUOUS, ULTIMATELY *SELF-DESTRUCTIVE* STRING OF HOMICIDES.

USUALLY AFTER SOME INCIDENT MAKES THEM... *"SNAP."* SAY, THE DEATH OF A *FRIEND...?*

THE SERIAL MURDERER, ON THE OTHER HAND, MAKES A LIFESTYLE, A *CAREER* OF STALKING VICTIMS. THEY NEVER STOP KILLING UNTIL THEY'RE *CAUGHT.*

SOUNDS FAMILIAR. YOU EVER HEAR OF A FELLA THEY CALL *RAILSPLITTER?*

OF COURSE. *TWENTY-SEVEN* VICTIMS OVER THE PAST TEN YEARS. THE BUREAU WOULD *LOVE* TO NAIL THE CREEP. WHY DO YOU--

WE'RE *HERE.*

BERKELY, I... I DON'T THINK THIS IS SUCH A GOOD *PLAN* ANYMORE...

COME ON, GIRL, SEE THIS THROUGH WITH ME! THIS HOSPITAL IS *CRAWLING* WITH MONSTERS! WE *BOTH* SAW THEM WITH OUR OWN EYES.

DID WE...?

WE'LL FORCE THEM TO *REVEAL* THEMSELVES, THE G-MAN WILL SEE, AND--

ANSWER MY *QUESTION,* BERKELY! *DID* YOU ACTUALLY *SEE* ANY MONSTERS HERE EARLIER? OR AT THE OLD LADY'S HOUSE?

...

NO, DEAR. ONLY THE ONES IN THE OFFICE--THE ONES I *KILLED.*

THEN, YOU *LIED* TO ME.

BECAUSE I *BELIEVE* IN YOU. AND THAT'S ALL THAT MATTERS.

NOW, I'M GOING TO GO IN THERE AND START *SHOOTING.* SURE WOULD BE DUCKY IF YOU'D MAKE SURE I CHOOSE THE RIGHT *TARGETS...*

YOU FEEL IT, TOO, DON'T YOU? YOU WERE *DRAWN* HERE.

Huh?

THIS IS WHERE THEY *DO* IT.

THIS IS WHERE THEY GET THEIR *INSTRUCTIONS!* WHERE THEY TALK TO THE *THING* THEY SERVE!

I SAW IT ALL--*AFTER* I DIED...

I WAS HOME ALONE WHEN I WENT INTO *LABOR.* SOMETHING WENT *WRONG.* BY THE TIME DOCTOR MASTIPHAL GOT THERE, IT WAS TOO LATE FOR *ME.*

HE COULDN'T *SEE* ME. OR MAYBE HE JUST DIDN'T *NOTICE* ME THERE...

I *WATCHED,* FROM UP ABOVE...HE CUT ME OPEN TO *SAVE* THE BABY.

I HEARD IT *CRYING.* EVERYTHING WAS OKAY. SO, WHY...

...WHY WAS HE FILLING OUT *TWO* DEATH CERTIFICATES...?

HE BROUGHT MY BABY HERE. HE AND DOC VERDELET AND SOME OTHERS *OFFERED* IT TO THEIR MASTER!

WHO WOULD EVER THINK SUCH THINGS *LIVED* HERE? *WORKED* RIGHT *HERE?*

HOLY GOD...

GOD ISN'T HERE. NOT IN *THIS* PLACE.

NO MORE... PLEASE, I DON'T WANT TO *KNOW...*

FORTY-ONE.

...WHAT...?

THE AGENT SAID I ONLY HAD TWENTY-SEVEN KILLS. IT'S FORTY-ONE. *MORE* IF YOU COUNT TONIGHT.

I WANT YOU TO *KNOW*, CASSIE. IT'S IMPORTANT YOU KNOW *ALL* OF IT NOW.

WHERE'D SHE *GO*...?

I *ALWAYS* HAD THESE FEELINGS... THESE *URGES*. IT'S WHY I *ENLISTED* IN THE FIRST PLACE--

-- FIGURED THE SERVICE WAS *MADE* FOR GUYS LIKE ME.

SURE ENOUGH, I MADE A WHIZ-BANG MARINE. BUT WHEN I CAME HOME FROM THE WAR, I DIDN'T *FIT IN*.

AND WHEN I COULDN'T HOLD IT IN ANY MORE, MY DADDY BECAME MY FIRST PEACETIME KILL.

I WONDERED EVER SINCE WHY I WAS *BORN* THIS WAY. WHAT *PURPOSE* WOULD THE GOOD LORD HAVE, PUTTING SUCH THINGS IN MY HEAD?

AND THEN I MEET *YOU*, AND SUDDENLY I *KNOW* MY PURPOSE. YOU CAN SEE THE *REAL* MONSTERS OUT THERE, BUT YOU LOOK AT *ME*, AND YOU *DON'T* SEE A BEAST.

YOU KNOW *WHY*, DON'T YOU? 'CAUSE WE'RE THE *SAME*, YOU AND I. WE WEREN'T MEANT TO FIT IN. WE WERE MEANT FOR SOMETHING GREATER.

WE'RE *HOLY SOLDIERS*, YOU AND I.

YOU'VE GOT THE *GRACE* TO *SPOT* THEM. I'VE GOT WHAT IT TAKES TO *END* THEM. WE'VE BEEN LOOKING FOR EACH OTHER ALL OUR LIVES AND NEVER KNEW IT.

YOU'RE... YOU'RE *RIGHT*.

NOW I HAVE A CONFESSION FOR *YOU*, BERKELY...

I WAS *WRONG* EARLIER. THAT N.B.I. AGENT? HE *WAS* ONE OF THEM. I WASN'T SURE UNTIL HE *RAN*...

THANKS. YOU CALLED FOR *BACKUP*?

YUP. SPEAKING OF WHICH, WHAT HAPPENED TO THEM *AGENTS* YOU HAD WITH YOU BEFORE--

BLAM
BLAM
BLAM
BLAM
BLAM
BLAM BLAM

"...WE'RE THE *SAME*, YOU AND I. WE WEREN'T *MEANT* TO FIT IN. WE WERE MEANT FOR SOMETHING *GREATER*."

WHO *IS* THIS GUY...?

I WASN'T *SURE*, FOR A WHILE THERE.

I THOUGHT THAT MAYBE HE WAS THE *MOTIVATOR* BEHIND HER KILLING SPREE, BUT *NO*...

...HE WAS JUST ANOTHER ONE OF HER *VICTIMS*.

Route
666

PATROLMAN
PERDITION
"ABANDON ALL HOPE"

CHAPTER 7

MISTER BARKSDALE--

MASTER-SERGEANT BARKSDALE--

RRRIGHT. I THINK I MIGHT KNOW A WAY TO *RESOLVE* YOUR CLAIM. JUST A SECOND...

DINNER IS HERE. SPECIAL DELIVERY.

SEND IT IN.

NOW, HERE'S WHAT I THINK YOU SHOULD DO...

TAKE THESE, AND ONCE YOU'RE INSIDE, YOU TELL MISS BYLETH *EVERYTHING* YOU TOLD ME.

RATHER THAN RISK EMBARRASSMENT IN FRONT OF THE *BOARD*, SHE'LL FIX YOUR TROUBLES ON THE SPOT.

MISS *BYLETH*. THAT'S THE BOSS-LADY?

JUST DON'T LET THEM KNOW *I* LET YOU IN, OKAY?

THANKS, MISSY. I *KNEW* IF I PUSHED HARD ENOUGH, I'D FIND ONE *DECENT HUMAN BEING* LEFT AROUND HERE.

...CASSIE...YOU PROMISED...

...→ahuh, ahuh←... →snff←...

...SO SORRY...→ahuh← ...I'M *SOO* SORRY... →ahuh←...

...I KNOW I'M THE *LAST* PERSON...YOU EVER WANTED TO SEE AGAIN...

...BUT YOU'RE THE *ONLY ONE* I COULD THINK OF WHO MIGHT *UNDERSTAND*... →SNFF←...

TELL ME ALL ABOUT IT WHILE YOU EAT. I WON'T CARE IF YOU TALK WITH YOUR MOUTH FULL.

THANKS. I'M *STARVING*...

RECKONED AS MUCH. SO WHAT EXACTLY *HAPPENED* IN STONE RIVER? 'CAUSE IF THE PAPERS HAVE IT RIGHT, THIS MIGHT JUST BE YOUR *LAST MEAL.*

AFTER I LEFT YOU AT THE CHURCH, I HOPPED A BOXCAR AND I MET A HOBO NAMED *BERKELY.*

HE NEVER DOUBTED A THING I TOLD HIM ABOUT THE *MONSTERS,* THE *GHOSTS...* THE WHOLE FREAKY MESS!

I THOUGHT I'D FOUND SOMEONE WHO REALLY *UNDERSTOOD* WHAT I'M UP AGAINST...

...AND WHEN WE FOUND EVEN *MORE* CREEPIES HIDING OUT IN STONE RIVER HOSPITAL, HE CONVINCED ME TO *GO AFTER* THEM.

→chompf← TURNS OUT HE WAS A *MURDERER.* PAPERS CALLED HIM...→ulp←... "RAILSPLITTER."

MY LITTLE WAR WAS JUST AN *EXCUSE* FOR HIM TO KILL MORE PEOPLE.

WORSE-- HE'D REALLY MADE ME FEEL LIKE WE WERE BOTH *THE SAME,* AND NOW...I CAN'T *SHAKE* THAT FEELING.

AM I JUST LIKE HIM? GOD KNOWS ENOUGH PEOPLE *DIE* WHEREVER I GO...

WHAT MAKES YOU THINK *I* CAN ANSWER THAT QUESTION? I MEAN...WHY COME TO ME INSTEAD OF YOUR *PARENTS?* THEY MUST BE SICK WITH WORRY--!

HOW COULD *THEY* UNDERSTAND? *YOU'VE* SEEN THE THINGS I'M FIGHTING--THE *WOLFMEN,* ANYWAY.

DIDN'T YOU...?

WELL...IT *WAS* DARK...

OH, NO YOU *DON'T!* DON'T YOU *LIE* TO ME... OR PATRONIZE ME, OR *WHATEVER...*

I'M HERE BECAUSE I *NEED* YOUR HONEST, PROFESSIONAL OPINION AS A *COP*...AS SOMEONE WHO CAN TAKE A GOOD HARD LOOK AT ME...

TELL ME, SHERIFF FERNANDEZ: *AM* I A KILLER? *AM* I LIKE BERKELY?!

BECAUSE THE FARTHER I GO... THE *LESS SENSE* ANY OF THIS MAKES. I DON'T SEEM TO KNOW...*WHO* I AM ANYMORE...AND I CAN'T DO THIS *ALONE...*

RINGGGG RINGGGG

wh... wha...?

VACANCY
NO VACANCY

MOTEL

TUMBLEWEED

RINGGGG

...wh... WAITASECOND...

MELCHIOR HERE.

WHO...?

Um...YES... YES, I *DID* GIVE HIM MY CARD. GO AHEAD AND PATCH HIM THROUGH...

SPECIAL AGENT GUNNAR MELCHIOR SPEAKING.

YES, I REMEMBER YOU. WHAT'S THIS ABOUT?

SHE'S *WHAT?!*

OKAY...OKAY, *KEEP* HER THERE. I CAN BE THERE IN LESS THAN TWO HOURS. I ASSUME SHE DOESN'T KNOW YOU'VE CALLED ME...?

UI'D *KELL* FIR A NAPKIN RAGHT ABOOT NOO...

YES, YOUR AGENT WILL REMAIN UNHARMED--PROVIDED HE HANDS HER OVER WITHOUT QUESTION.

VERY GOOD, MISTER PURVIS. THE ADVERSARY WILL SEE TO YOUR *REWARD* ONCE WE RENDER HER UNTO HIM.

NO, I DON'T THINK *PRESIDENT* IS OUT OF THE QUESTION.

GOODBYE.

SERVIETTE...?

CHEERS, LASS.

THE STARKWEATHER GIRL IS IN CUSTODY. WE SHALL *COLLECT* HER FROM THE LOCAL AUTHORITIES AND PERSONALLY *ESCORT* HER BACK TO PERDITION.

KEEP IN MIND THAT THE GIRL MUST ARRIVE *ALIVE.* THE ADVERSARY WISHES TO EXAMINE HER HIMSELF.

AYE, AN' SENCE *WHEN* DAE CONSTABLES SURRENDER PRESONERS TAE *INSURANCE EXECUTIVES,* BYLETH?

THEY'LL THINK WE'RE N.B.I. AGENTS. IT SHOULD ALL GO QUICKLY AND QUIETLY.

AN' FIR THIS YE NEED THE *ENTIRE* BOORD O' DIRECTORS?! WHY DRAG *ME* ALOONG, IF I CANNAE HAVE A *SQUARE GO* AT ANYONE...

...OR AT LEAST SINK ME WEE *FANGS* IN A THROAT OR TAE? 'TIS A WEST O' *TALENT!*

⇒SIGH⇐... BRAATHWAATE, IF I EVER FIND OUT THE HUMANS IN YOUR "*WEE*" DISTRICT *DON'T* REALLY SPEAK WITH THAT LUDICROUS *ACCENT...*

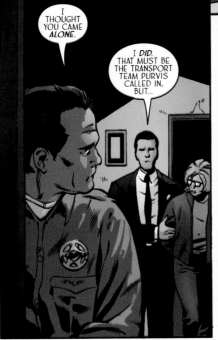

I THOUGHT YOU CAME *ALONE.*

I *DID.* THAT MUST BE THE TRANSPORT TEAM PURVIS CALLED IN, BUT...

...I DIDN'T THINK THEY'D BE HERE SO *SOON...*

HELLO...?

JUST ONE MONTH AWAY...

EDGE 11

Other Worlds Are Waiting For You

CROSSGEN
GRAPHIC NOVELS

If you're new to the CrossGen Compendia, chances are there are plenty of great stories you have yet to read. Never fear! It's not too late to jump on board any one of our exciting series.

Even if you can't find back issues of FORGE or EDGE, every one of CrossGen's series gets collected into Graphic Novels, available through your local comic shop, bookstore, or online bookseller. Every Graphic Novel we've published to date are described on the following pages, and there are a lot more to come in 2003!

Whether you're looking for that missing masterpiece or just want a handy collection of your favorite series you can return to again and again, CrossGen has the Graphic Novel for you.

Bon Appetit!

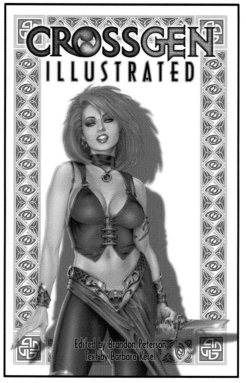

CrossGen
Illustrated v.1

This deluxe illustrated introduction to the
many worlds of the CrossGen Universe
brings together the talents of all your
favorite CrossGen artists with insightful
commentary and additional information.
It's the best of the best art produced
by CrossGen, packaged to appeal to
long-time fans and new readers alike!

ISBN 1-931484-05-8
192 pgs. • $24.95

CROSSGEN
GRAPHIC NOVELS

The Path v.1: Crisis of Faith

Writer: Ron Marz
Penciler: Bart Sears
Inker: Mark Pennington
Colorist: Michael Atiyeh

Set on an exotic world akin to feudal Japan, THE PATH tells the story of a man stripped of his faith by not only the gods to whom he prays, but the emperor he is honor-bound to serve. When the monk Obo-san witnesses the death of his brother at the hands of the gods, he swears to have his vengeance by using the gods' own Weapon of Heaven against them. Meanwhile, the emperor teeters on the brink of madness and threatens to lead the nation to ruin. Torn between duty and destiny, Obo-san defies the Emperor and finds himself a wanted man, and not even the all-powerful weapon he possesses can save him.

ISBN 1-931484-32-5
192 pgs. • $19.95

CROSSGEN
GRAPHIC NOVELS

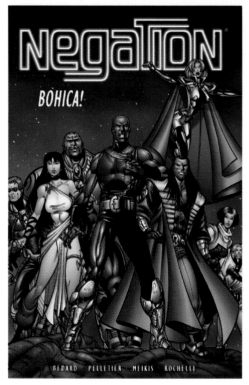

Negation v.1: Bohica!

Writer: Tony Bedard
Penciler: Paul Pelletier
Inker: Dave Meikis
Colorist: James Rochelle

Beyond the dimensional rift exists an evil known as the Negation, an empire bent on expanding into our reality. They have kidnapped an array of beings from across the CrossGen Universe, condemning them to a prison planet where their strengths and weaknesses can be probed. Lost and without a clue, a small group nevertheless breaks free of their gulag. They manage to escape under the dubious leadership of Obregon Kaine, a human being without any special powers or abilities that somehow forges them into a team. Kaine convinces them that the only way home is to find, corner, and defeat Charon, the godlike leader of the Negation Empire. It's *The Great Escape* meets *The Dirty Dozen* in a galaxy far, far away.

ISBN 1-931484-30-9
192 pgs. • $19.95

Ruse v.1:
Enter the Detective

Writer: Mark Waid
Penciler: Butch Guice
Inker: Mike Perkins
Colorist: Laura DePuy

The world no longer holds any mysteries for Simon Archard, the greatest detective of his age. The stupidity of the common criminal, the ease with which he's caught, the paltry stakes of the game — all of it has pushed Archard to the verge of retirement. Then a mysterious new menace takes the stage, a hideous evil playing for very high stakes indeed. Aided by his beautiful and charming assistant, Emma Bishop, Archard embarks on the case of his career. RUSE is an ongoing duel of warring masterminds held under the cold glow of gaslights.

ISBN 1-931484-19-8
160 pgs. • $15.95

RUSE
ENTER THE DETECTIVE

WAID · GUICE · PERKINS · DEPUY

CROSSGEN
GRAPHIC NOVELS

Sojourn v.1:
From the Ashes

Writer: Ron Marz
Penciler: Greg Land
Inker: Drew Geraci
Colorist: Caesar Rodriguez

Hundreds of years ago, the Five Lands joined together to end the tyranny of Mordath. Now a mysterious force has brought him back from the dead. With a troll army at his back, Mordath soon puts the Five Lands under his heel. Only one woman has eluded his iron grip. SOJOURN is the story of Arwyn, a woman whose one aim is to slay Mordath. But to do that she must first find the weapon that can kill a man who is already dead.

ISBN 1-931484-15-5
192 pgs. • $19.95

Sojourn v.2:
The Dragon's Tale

Writer: Ron Marz
Penciler: Greg Land
Inker: Drew Geraci
Colorist: Caesar Rodriguez

Arwyn's quest begins in earnest as she searches for the first of the Five Fragments in a dragon's treasure hoard. But a beast as powerful as a dragon might represent a quick route to Mordath's destruction… if the creature can be harnessed.

ISBN 1-931484-34-1
160 pgs. • $15.95

CROSSGEN
GRAPHIC NOVELS

Crux v.1:
Atlantis Rising

Writer: Mark Waid
Penciler: Steve Epting
Inker: Rick Magyar
Colorist: Frank D'Armata

Millennia ago, the Atlanteans were the self-styled mentors to the newborn race known as *homo sapiens*. But when a mysterious cataclysm plunged Atlantis and its people beneath the waves, six — and only six — awoke one thousand centuries later to find their island city forgotten and in ruins, their brothers and sisters caught in an unshakeable slumber...and Earth devoid of all life. Now the one, simple question that drives them is this: Whatever happened to the human race?

ISBN 1-931484-14-7
160 pgs. • $15.95

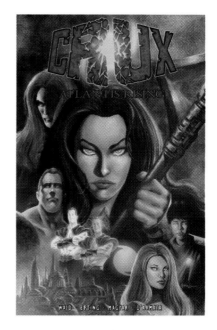

Crux v.2:
Test of Time

Writer: Mark Waid
Penciler: Steve Epting
Inker: Rick Magyar
Colorist: Frank D'Armata

Wandering the remains of an abandoned future Earth, the Atlanteans must contend with the warrior forces of the Negation, a terrifying and ruthless extradimensional race. Their only hope of survival is find the long-lost human race — but every exploratory mission simply takes them further into danger.

ISBN 1-931484-36-8
160 pgs. • $15.95

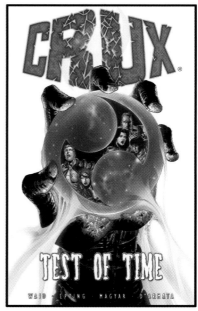

CROSSGEN
GRAPHIC NOVELS

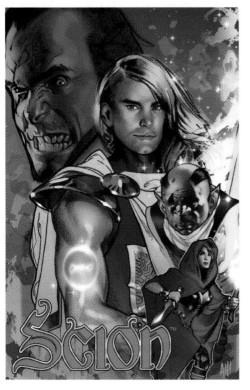

Scion v.1:
Conflict of Conscience

Writer: Ron Marz
Penciler: Jim Cheung
Inker: Don Hillsman II
Colorist: Caesar Rodriquez

SCION is the story of Ethan, youngest
prince of an ancient empire locked in an
uneasy truce with its Eastern rivals. In an
age in which ritual combat has taken the
place of real war, Ethan prepares to mark
his passage into manhood by participating in
his first tournament. Then an incident occurs
which changes his life forever — and leads to
the first open warfare in generations. Young,
headstrong, and somewhat naïve, Ethan
embarks on a quest to avenge his brother's
death that takes him deep into the heart of
the Eastern lands. This is a world where
dragons are scientifically engineered creatures
with on-board computers, hovercraft are
decked out like tall ships, and Lesser Races
are bred for toil.

ISBN 1-931484-02-3
192 pgs. • $19.95

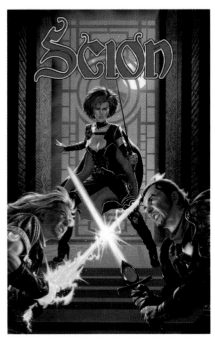

Scion v.2: Blood for Blood

Writer: Ron Marz
Penciler: Jim Cheung
Inker: Don Hillsman II
Colorist: Caesar Rodriquez & Justin Ponsor

Full-scale war has erupted between the Raven and
Heron dynasties. Among the first casualties was
Prince Artor, Ethan's oldest brother and heir to
the throne, who was brutally slain by Raven Prince
Bron. Swearing vengeance, Ethan has set out on
a journey that leads to the very heart of Raven
power, and a battle with Bron that will leave only
one man standing.

ISBN 1-931484-08-2
208 pgs. • $19.95

Scion v.3:
Divided Loyalties

Writer: Ron Marz
Penciler: Jim Cheung
Inker: Don Hillsman II
Colorist: Justin Ponsor

The war continues to rage in the latest SCION
trade paperback. Ethan sees first-hand the
sufferings of the genetically engineered Lesser
Races and is forced to choose between his loyalty
to his family and his loyalty to a greater good.
His decision is not only unexpected, it may
well determine the course of history for his
entire world.

ISBN 1-931484-26-0
176 pgs. • $15.95

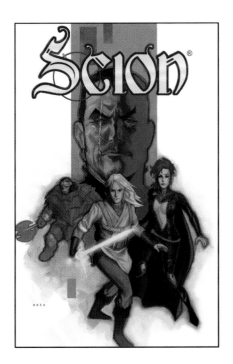

CROSSGEN
GRAPHIC NOVELS

Sigil v.1: Mark of Power

Writer: Barbara Kesel
Penciler: Ben Lai
Inker: Ray Lai
Colorist: Wil Quintana

Samandahl Rey was a loner, a wandering
ex-soldier whose sense of responsibility
extended only to himself and to his friend,
Roiya Sintor — until the Sigil was forced
upon him, a brand of vast power that
changed his destiny forever. Now the first
daughter of Delassia needs his protection,
his worst enemy is about to ask for his help,
and the entire Planetary Union is depending
on Sam to free its citizens from the tyranny
of the vile, lizardlike Saurian race. Sam's
about to find he had no idea what the
word 'responsibility' meant.

ISBN 1-931484-01-5
192 pgs. • $19.95

Sigil v.2:
The Marked Man

Writer: Barbara Kesel
Penciler: Scot Eaton
Inker: Andrew Hennessy
Colorist: Wil Quintana

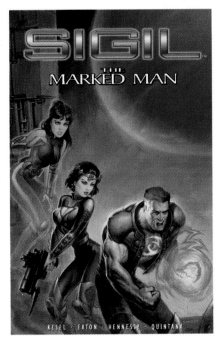

On the run from the Saurian Empire and Sam's personal enemy, the Saurian Prince Tchlusarud, Sam and Roiya are headed 'anywhere but here.' Tagging along is Zanniati, the runaway wife of the Sultan Ronolo of Tanipal, and JeMerik Meer, a member of the Sultan's guard. They end up in Delassia, where they discover Zanni's more than just a trophy wife, and Roiya discovers there's more to JeMerik than just a rouguish smile and good timing.

ISBN 1-931484-07-4
208 pgs. • $19.95

Sigil v.3:
The Lizard God

Writer: Mark Waid
Penciler: Scot Eaton
Inker: Andrew Hennessy
Colorist: Wil Quintana

Finally, after hundreds of years, the interstellar war between the human race and the reptilian warriors known as the Saurians has come to a head. Humanity has launched a last-ditch offensive led by Samandahl Rey, a blue-collar soldier-of-fortune branded with the Sigil of Power, the universe's greatest weapon. Victory is assured — until Rey suddenly finds himself mysteriously transported to another world. Now he must find his way back home — and fast — before the entire galaxy falls under Saurian rule.

ISBN 1-931484-28-7
160 pgs. • $15.95

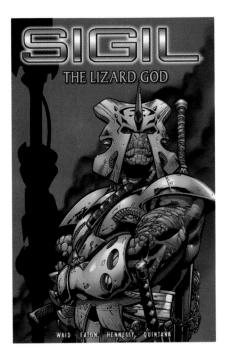

CROSSGEN
GRAPHIC NOVELS

The First v.1: Two Houses Divided

Writer: Barbara Kesel
Penciler: Bart Sears
Inker: Andy Smith
Colorist: Michael Atiyeh

The First is a race of godlike beings that believe they formed themselves in a passion of creation. Their past lost in a fog of myth, their present is a comfortable routine — until a new power emerges that could topple their preeminence. Faced with its first true threat, their society begins to fall apart, and soon the mystery of the Sigil-Bearers threatens to plunge the First into civil war.

ISBN 1-931484-04-X
192 pgs. • $19.95

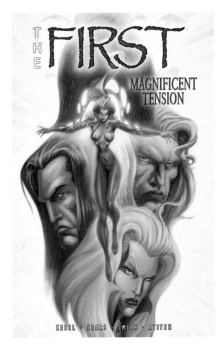

The First v.2: Magnificent Tension

Writer: Barbara Kesel
Penciler: Bart Sears
Inker: Andy Smith
Colorist: Michael Atiyeh

The gods of the CrossGen Universe are in the process of being deposed from that self-proclaimed role because of the creation of the Sigil-Bearers. Anxiety over these powerful new arrivals has ruptured the fault lines in the social structure of the First, causing Ingra, Leader of House Sinister, to make a bold move to launch her planned takeover of House Dexter. Seahn has collected together the unhappy second-born, ready to demand that they be given equal status to the First. Persha, Ingra's daughter, sneaks over to House Dexter to meet Pyrem, her father and Leader of that House. And Gannish the Truthseeker learns a frightening truth about the reality of the First.

ISBN 1-931484-17-1
192 pgs. • $19.95

The First v.3: Sinister Motives

Writer: Barbara Kesel
Penciler: Andrea Di Vito
Inker: Rob Hunter
Colorist: Rob Schwager

When gods break their vows, death is certain to follow. In the land of the First, dissent has erupted into open warfare. Seahn, young turk of House Dexter, has forsaken his ideals and his House to find power on the other side. Both sides are caught up in a tide of emotion and eruption of old hatreds. War seems inevitable. But war isn't what two manipulative mentors have in mind for the gods of the CrossGen Universe, as they take a direct hand in altering the course of history.

ISBN 1-931484-39-2
160 pgs.• $15.95

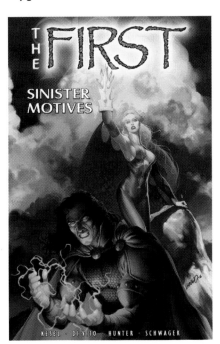

CROSSGEN
GRAPHIC NOVELS

Mystic v.1:
Rite of Passage

Writer: Ron Marz
Penciler: Brandon Peterson
Inker: John Dell
Colorist: Andrew Crossley

Ciress is a world that runs on magic, and
those with the most magic run the world.
Genevieve Villard was in line to become a
great leader, but during her Rite of Ascension
something went horribly wrong. Her sister
Giselle, a flibbertigibbet society girl, was
conferred not only the power that was rightly
Genevieve's but that of every other Guild
Master on Ciress. Now Giselle must come to
terms with being the magical protector of her
entire planet — if the Guild Masters let her
live that long. Vibrant color and lush detail
brings the magic of MYSTIC to life each
month, as Giselle learns to live with her
strange new power and the responsibility
that goes with it.

ISBN 1-931484-00-7
192 pgs. • $19.95

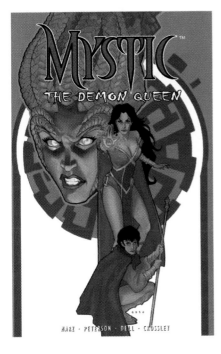

Mystic v.2:
The Demon Queen

Writer: Ron Marz
Penciler: Brandon Peterson
Inker: John Dell
Colorist: Andrew Crossley

The second volume of MYSTIC introduces Animora, a demon queen brought back to life in a dubious scheme of the Guild Masters to regain their powers. They swiftly learn what it is to make a deal with a devil, as Animora double-crosses the Guild Masters and threatens to enslave all Ciress. Only the power of Giselle's mysterious sigil and the combined wisdom of the Guild Spirits can stop Animora's evil.

ISBN 1-931484-06-6
208 pgs. • $19.95

Mystic v.3:
Siege of Scales

Writer: Ron Marz & Tony Bedard
Penciler: Brandon Peterson
Inker: John Dell
Colorist: Andrew Crossley

The Demon Queen Animora is making her own bid for supremacy. Witness the final showdown between Giselle and Animora in this third volume of the MYSTIC series.

ISBN 1-931484-24-4
160 pgs. • $15.95

Meridian v.1: Flying Solo

Writer: Barbara Kesel
Penciler: Joshua Middleton
& Steve McNiven
Inker: Dexter Vines
Colorist: Michael Atiyeh

MERIDIAN is the story of Sephie of the island city of Meridian, a sheltered young girl with a fairy tale life. Her father, the Minister of Meridian, dies, and she inherits a sigil imbued with the power to create. So does her wicked uncle Ilahn, except that his powers are bent on destruction and domination. Sephie finds herself at the center of a power struggle. Kidnapped to the city of Cadador, Sephie's journey home to Meridian puts her in the path of many people good and bad that help her grow up and counter Ilahn's plans to take over her world.

ISBN 1-931484-03-1
192 pgs. • $19.95

Meridian v.2: Going to Ground

Writer: Barbara Kesel
Penciler: Steve McNiven
Inker: Tom Simmons
Colorist: Morry Hollowell

Meridian is ravaged by the occupying forces from Cadador. The Minister of Meridian, Sephie, has survived a trial by fire. Returning home, Sephie will use the strange healing powers she's been given to banish the Cadadorians from her island. Unfortunately, her uncle Ilahn was also given a sigil and its wonderful ability to manipulate energies — but his power destroys.

ISBN 1-931484-09-0
208 pgs. • $19.95

Meridian v.3:
Taking the Skies

Writer: Barbara Kesel
Penciler: Steve McNiven
Inker: Tom Simmons
Colorist: Morry Hollowell

In this volume, Sephie takes to piracy to disrupt the trade routes Ilahn controls, but discovers that his own power extends beyond energy into the politics of contracts and influence. In a fight between two people given godlike powers, who wins?

ISBN 1-931484-21-X
160 pgs. • $15.95

Meridian v.4:
Coming Home

Writer: Barbara Kesel
Penciler: Steve McNiven
Inker: Tom Simmons
Colorist: Morry Hollowell

Aided by her band of freedom fighters, the Pirates of the Wind, Sephie fights to liberate Meridian. Awaiting her is a fateful showdown with Ilahn, a showdown that will cost Sephie her innocence and perhaps even her life. "Beautiful art and strong scripting make *Meridian* a superior value."
–*Publishers Weekly*

ISBN 1-931484-38-4
160 pgs. • $15.95

Q: What can you still buy
for three cents?

A: Thousands of pages of comics at
www.comicsontheweb.com